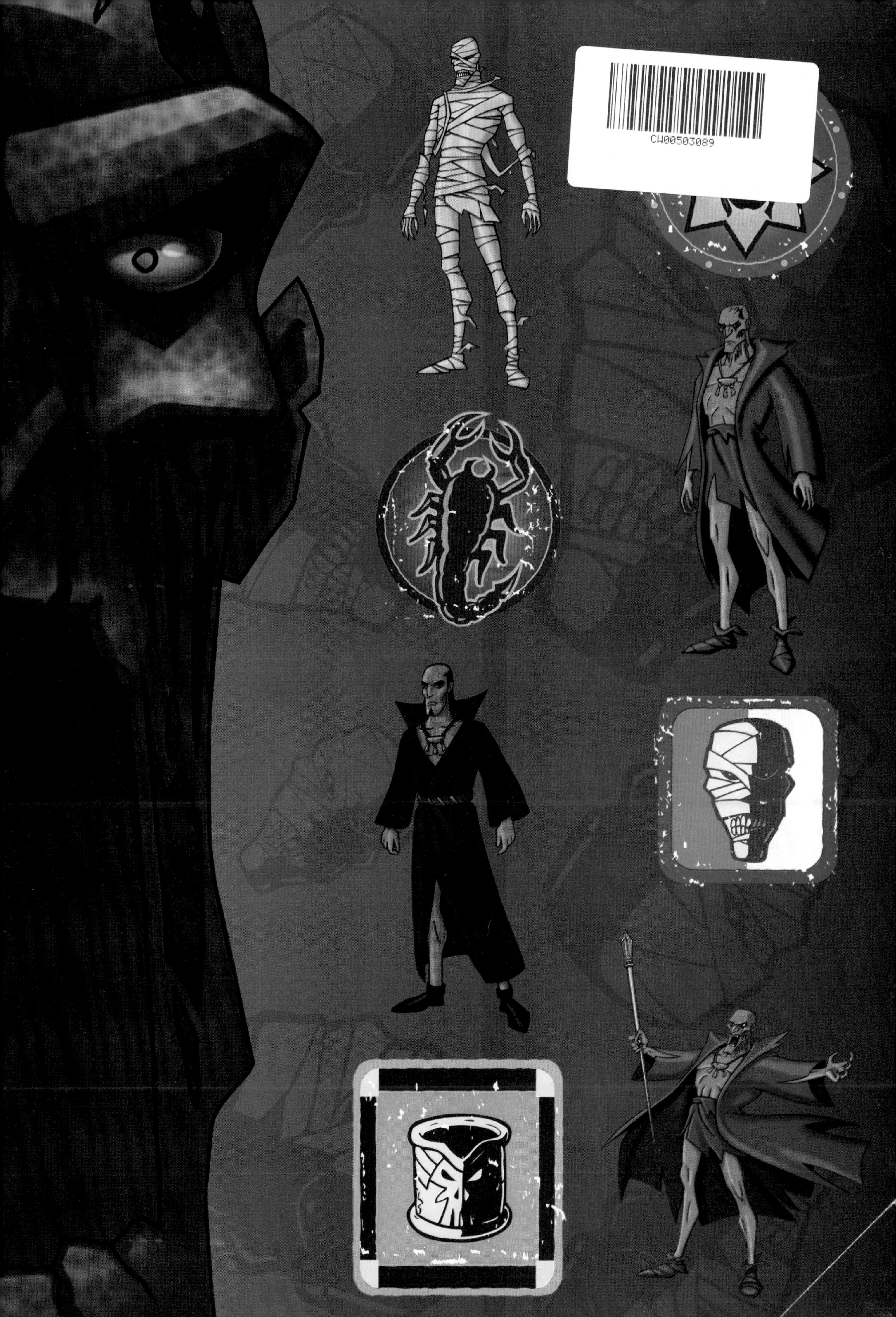

THE MUMMY™ CONTENTS

Published by Pedigree Books Limited
The Old Rectory, Matford Lane, Exeter EX2 4PS
E-mail books@pedigreegroup.co.uk
Published in 2002

THE STORY

IN THE BEGINNING...

Over 75 years ago, in 1925, a young American called Rick O'Connell and his wife-to-be, Evelyn Carnahan, began a sequence of events that now threatens the safety of the world. They discovered the secret of Hamunaptra, the Egyptian City of the Dead, and unleashed a monster with terrifying powers – Imhotep, the Mummy!
3215 years earlier, during the reign of Seti the First, Imhotep had been High Priest of The Dead in Thebes, the capital of Ancient Egypt. The Egyptian King, or Pharaoh, was engaged to marry the beautiful Anck-su-namun – but she loved Imhotep! When Seti discovered the couple together, Anck-su-namun killed herself in the knowledge that, one day, Imhotep could use his Book of the Dead to bring her back to life. But the furious Pharaoh ordered a terrible death for Imhotep. He was mummified and buried alive with hundreds of black scarab beetles starting to eat him. This Hom Dai, or half-death, meant that if Imhotep was ever disturbed, he would come back to life to inflict the same punishment on the rest of the world. The scarabs would fly again and turn everyone into his mummies!

This threat was so real and so terrible that a special group of soldiers called the Med-Jai dedicated themselves to guarding Hamunaptra for all time. So, when Rick and Evelyn arrived with her brother, Jonathan, to search the City of The Dead, the Med-Jai attacked them. But they failed to stop the visitors opening the tombs and releasing Imhotep. The Mummy was now on the loose! Knowing how disastrous this could be, the leader

SO FAR

of the modern Med-Jai, Ardeth Bay, changed sides and fought alongside the Europeans as they all struggled to contain Imhotep.
After many nail-biting adventures, terrifying fights and narrow escapes, the forces of darkness were finally contained. Just when all seemed lost, Evelyn used the sacred book of Amun Ra to summon the Egyptian god, Anubis. He took away Imhotep's supernatural powers and so, mere mortal again, Rick was able to kill the Mummy with his sword. But, as he died for a second time, Imhotep whispered some chilling words.

"THIS IS NOT THE END!"

THEN...

A few years later, in 1935, Rick and Evelyn were back in Egypt. Now married, and with an eight-year-old son Alex, they were excavating a tomb when they made an exciting find. It was a box with a mysterious Scorpion's head on it. And inside was a beautiful gold armband.

"It's the Bracelet of Anubis, the God of the Dead," gasped Evelyn. Little did they know what another ancient secret was about to be unleashed!
The Scorpion King, who once wore this golden bracelet, had been asleep in the diamond-topped Pyramid of Anubis for 6,000 years. But legend said, in the Year of the Scorpion, he would return and destroy the world with the terrifying dog-headed soldiers of Anubis. And 1935 was the Year of The Scorpion!

News of this event had already reached a red-robed criminal band led by Lock-Nah and a beautiful woman called Meela. She was Imhotep's lover, Anck-su-namun, in modern form and she had the Book Of The Dead. They were already in Hamunaptra, using the book to raise Imhotep once again. Their plan was to kill the Scorpion King and then use his army of Anubis to take over the world. Young Alex O'Connell thwarted their plan. The Bracelet of Anubis, which they needed to release the Scorpion King, was locked on his arm.
So they kidnapped the boy and took him to Egypt. The O'Connells and Jonathan followed in a rickety old balloon owned by Rick's friend, Izzy.
With the ever faithful Ardeth Bay helping them, it was a race against time to rescue Alex and prevent the Mummy from gaining such terrible powers that he could not be stopped.

Again, after a series of breathtaking chases, exciting escapades and split-second escapes, the O'Connells and their friends found themselves at the secret Pyramid of Anubis. Then tragedy struck! Appearing from nowhere, Meela stabbed Evelyn and killed her. But, instead of just grieving, Alex got hold of the Book of the Dead. With his father battling against the newly released Scorpion King, he brought his mother back to life!

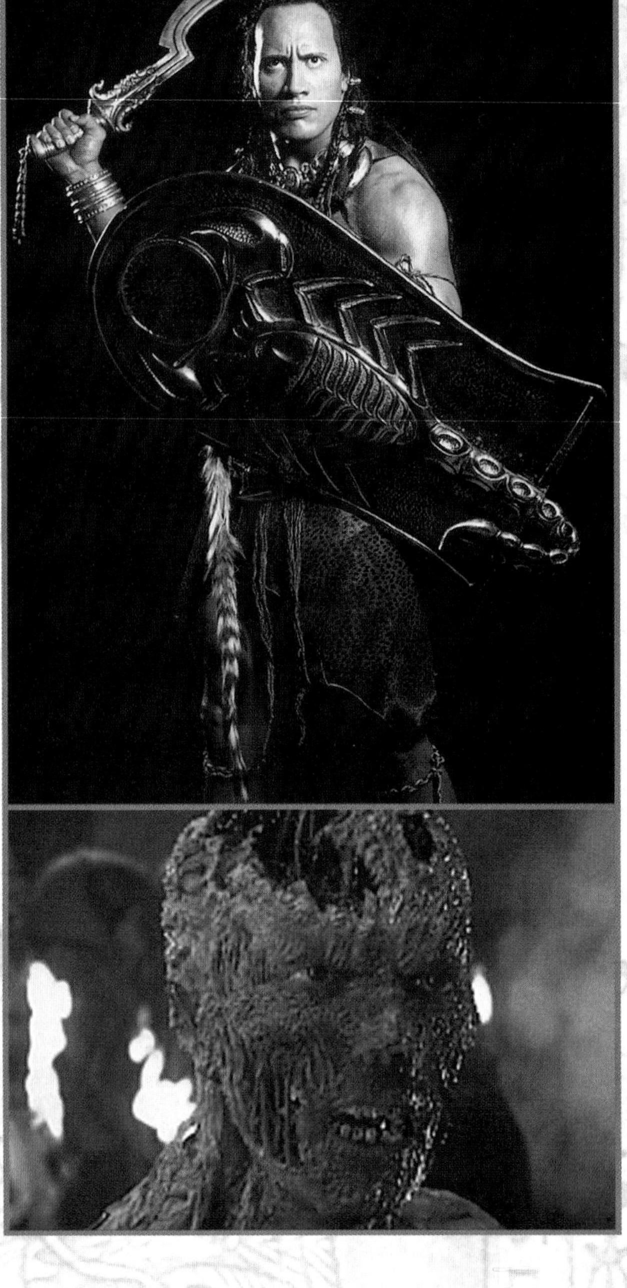

Now Evelyn came into her own. Realising that she was a descendent of Nefereri, the daughter of Seti the First, Evelyn used the knowledge and fighting skills she had inherited to defeat Meela. Then a golden spear that Jonathan was carrying was used to kill the Scorpion King. This returned the army of Anubis to the sands from which they came. Turning, Evelyn then read from the Book of Amun Ra, turning Imhotep back to mortal form again. Now Rick was able to kill both Meela and the Mummy so they would trouble the world no more. Or would they?

AND NOW...

It is 1938. Alex is 11. And he has another Ancient Egyptian bracelet locked round his wrist! It is the all-powerful Manacle Of Osiris. In order to get the bracelet off, the O'Connells must travel round the world in search of the sacred Scrolls Of Thebes. But they have a rival! Imhotep has returned for a third time and wants both the Manacle and the Scrolls in order to use their astonishing supernatural powers.

CAN THE MUMMY BE STOPPED FROM TAKING OVER THE WORLD?

IMHOTEP

THE MUMMY!

Dedicated to evil and world domination, he has three times the strength of a normal human. He also has special powers that allow him to raise small objects just by pointing at them or release deadly energy bolts from his fingertips. Most terrifying of all, however, is his knowledge of ancient Egyptian rituals and magic that summon up powers from the World Of The Undead!

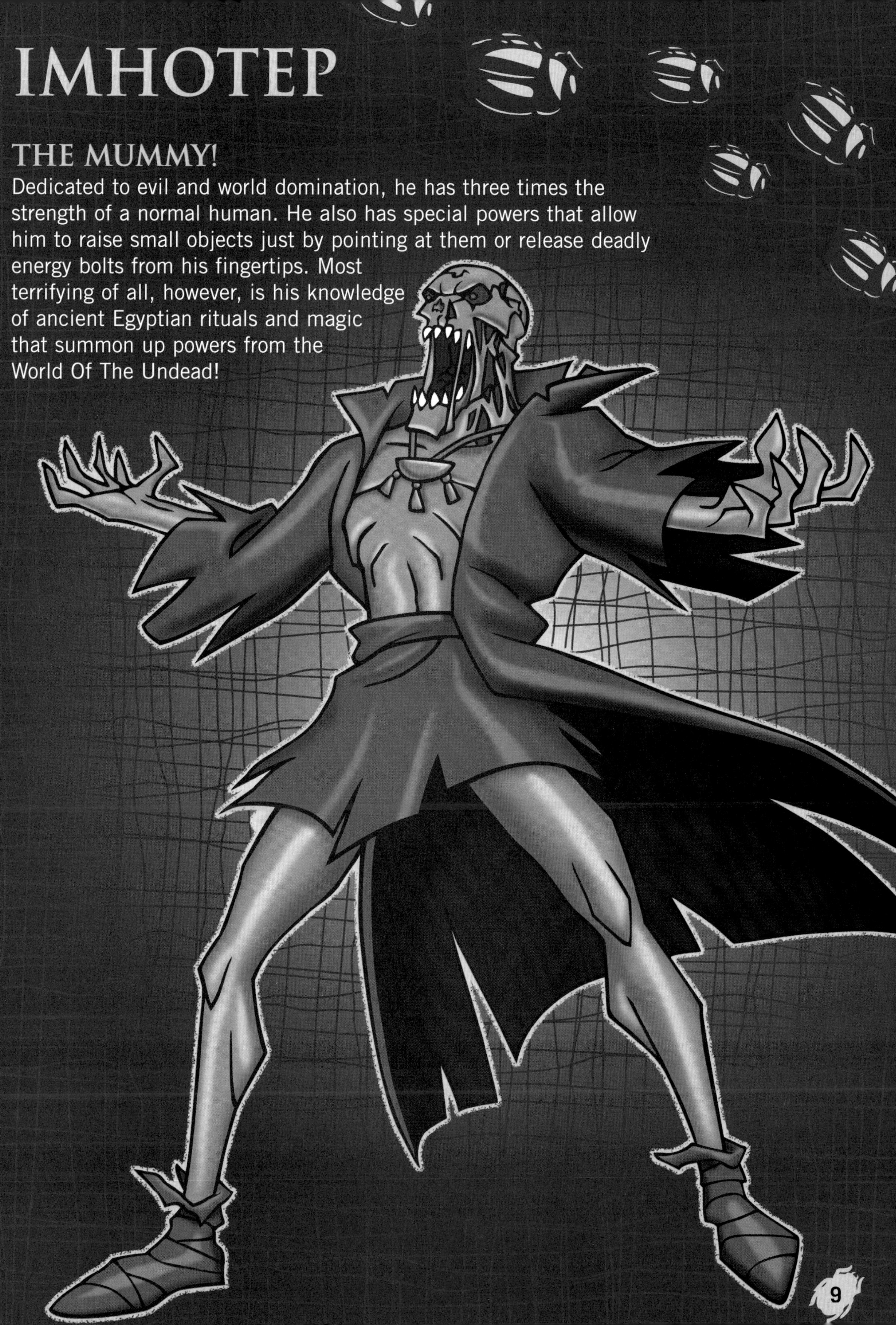

THE O'CONNELL FAMILY

RICK

Handsome, charming, funny and always cool under pressure, Rick O'Connell is a man of action who has travelled the world and seen it all. His verdict? Use your fists first and ask questions afterwards! A loving husband and a proud father, Rick would take any risk to protect his family.

EVELYN

Nowadays known to everyone as Evy, Mrs. O'Connell is still fuelled by the same thirst for knowledge that led her to Egypt in the first place. Educated, clever and strong-willed, Evy usually gets her own way and can battle with the best of them against the hostile forces of the Undead.

ALEX

Ever since he was old enough to read, Alex has shared his mother's passion for all things Egyptian. By now he has considerable knowledge of ancient languages and Egyptian history. He has also inherited his father's sense of humour and love of adventure which often gets him into trouble!

ARDETH BAY, TUT THE MONGOOSE AND THE ZEPHYR

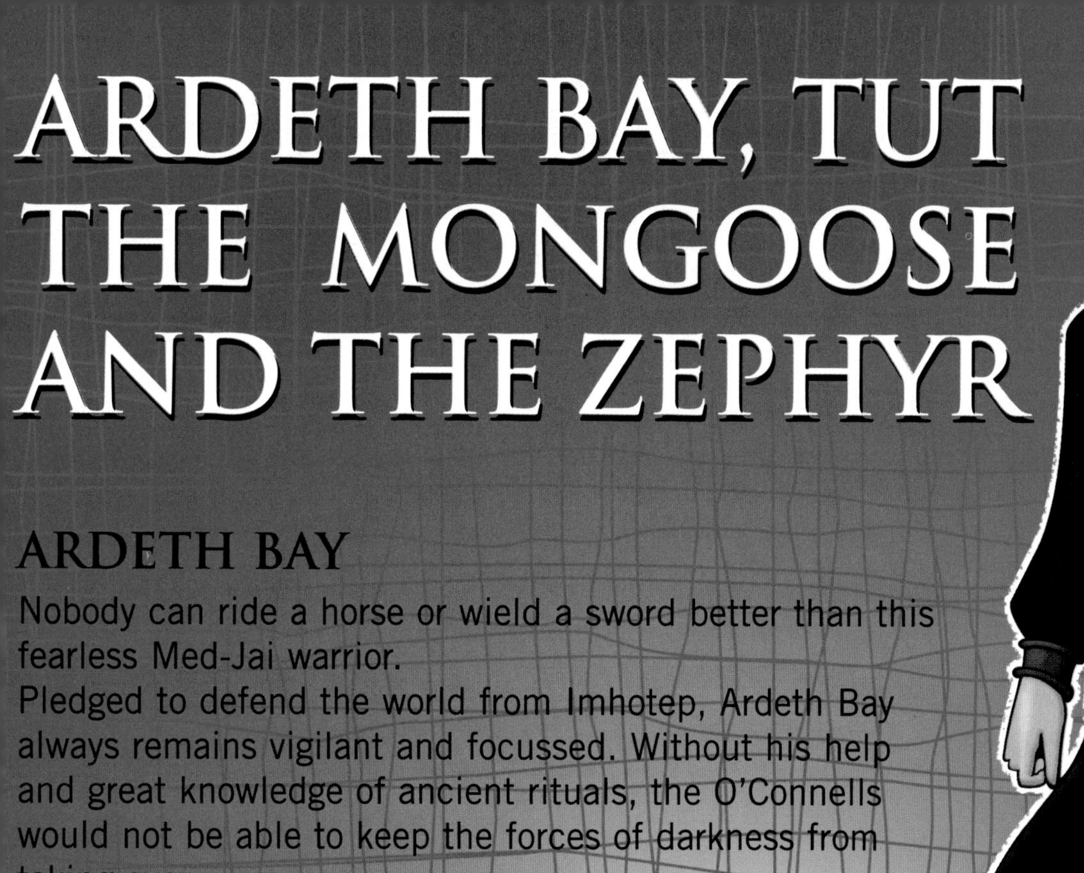

ARDETH BAY

Nobody can ride a horse or wield a sword better than this fearless Med-Jai warrior.
Pledged to defend the world from Imhotep, Ardeth Bay always remains vigilant and focussed. Without his help and great knowledge of ancient rituals, the O'Connells would not be able to keep the forces of darkness from taking over.

TUT

Alex's pet mongoose is even more fearless and brave than his master. Sometimes he gets Alex into trouble. More often than not, however, he gets his best friend out of trouble!

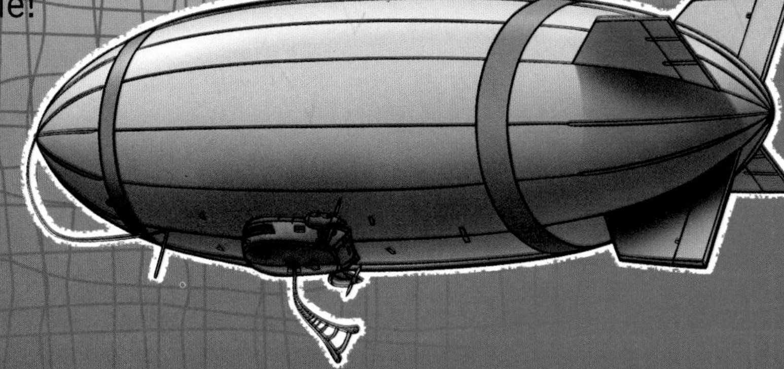

AND FINALLY...THE ZEPHYR

This is the O'Connells' main method of transport and often their mobile home. On loan from Evy's employer, The British Museum of Antiquities, the high-flying balloon (properly known as a 'dirigible') can fly to every corner of the world.

EVY'S PHARAOH-SIZE

This is a king-size puzzle - only Egyptian!

Evy O'Connell has set a challenge for you. All these words are connected with her beloved Egypt. Can you find them all in the grid and cross them off? They are spelt in all directions, including backwards.
When you have finished, there will be 11 letters left over. Transfer them, in order, into the box below the grid. What famous Egyptian name do they spell?

CHARIOT
PHARAOH
NILE
DIG
HIEROGLYPH
SWORD
RA
GISA
SCARAB BEETLE
DUNES
ANUBIS
SPHINX
SARCOPHAGUS
TOMB
SUN
NEFERTITI
SOUL
MUMMY
DESERT
GODS
PYRAMID
SPEAR
AFTERLIFE
SAND
CLEOPATRA

WORDSEARCH

S P H I N X D N A S H E
U S C T L U R A E P S L
N A A L M U M M Y S C T
T E F R E A O L N I H E
K H F T C O G S A B A E
D I G E E O P I M U R B
I R D O R R P A S N I B
M N O E D T L H T A O A
A R I W S S I I A R T R
R H A L S E E T F G A A
Y D U N E S R N I E U C
P H A R A O H T O M B S

_ _ _ _ _ _ _ _ _ _ _

Answer: TUTANKHAMEN

ARDETH BAY'S RIDD

Ardeth Bay, leader of the Med-Jai guards, is no stranger to riddles. His secret movement, dedicated to keeping The Mummy contained for all time, works through a system of signs and symbols designed to exclude strangers and speak only to the faithful.

Here are three clever riddles that disguise the names of people and places important to the Ancient Egyptians. Can you work out what they are?

1. Where am I ?

My first is in tea, in train and in toe,
My second's in heat and also in hoe.
My third is in egg and also in red,
My fourth is in bag, in ball and in bed.
My fifth is in eel, but never in hand,
My last is in sunshine, silver and sand.

_ _ _ _ _ _

LES OF THE SANDS

2. What am I ?

My first is in space and also in Spain,
My second's in peas and also in pain.
My third is in house and always in home,
My fourth is in icicle but never in gnome.
My fifth is in name and also in knot
And my last is a letter that marks the spot!

_ _ _ _ _ _

3. Who am I ?

My first is in find and also in ink,
My second's in mole, in mouse and in mink.
My third's not in bread, but is in howl,
My fourth is in open and also in owl.
My fifth is in tent, in towel and in tear,
My sixth is in feather, flower and fear.
My last is in poppy and also in pearl
And my whole name strikes terror all over the world!

_ _ _ _ _ _ _

Answers: 1.THEBES 2.SPHINX 3.IMHOTEP

THE MUMMY™

THE ANIMATED SERIES

'THE SUMMONING'

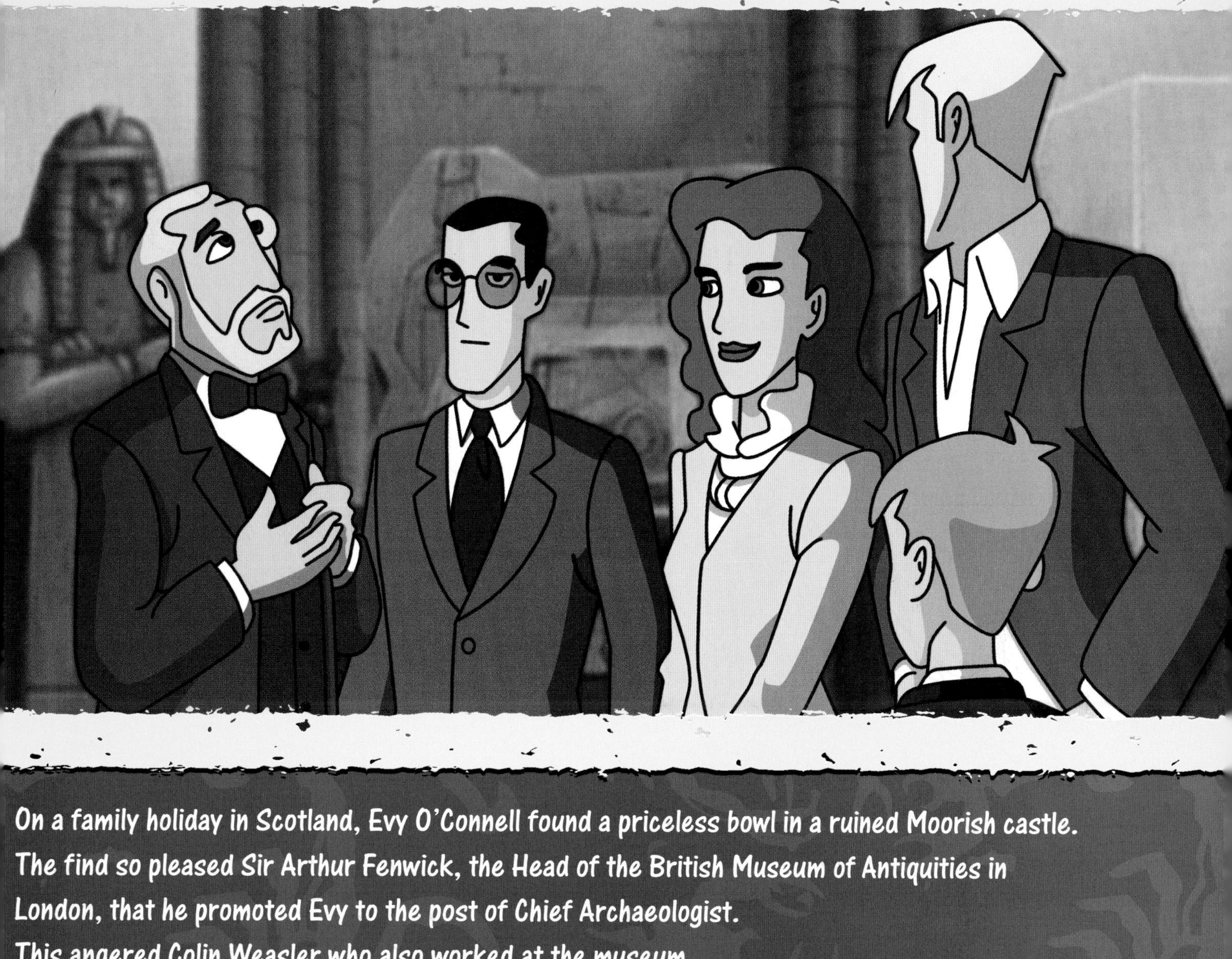

On a family holiday in Scotland, Evy O'Connell found a priceless bowl in a ruined Moorish castle. The find so pleased Sir Arthur Fenwick, the Head of the British Museum of Antiquities in London, that he promoted Evy to the post of Chief Archaeologist.

This angered Colin Weasler who also worked at the museum.

'That job was supposed to be mine!' he cried, storming off.

'I thought he took that rather well,' joked Rick.

As a result of the promotion, Evy and her family were sent to Egypt. A major dig was taking place at Hamunaptra, the City of the Dead, and Evy's job was to oversee it.

'Be at the airfield tomorrow at seven a.m.' said Sir Arthur. 'Your new transportation will be waiting for you.'

The vehicle was a dirigible - a huge, propeller-powered balloon with a cabin underneath.

'It's called The Zephyr,' said Evy.

'Can I fly it?' asked Alex.

'I don't believe they issue eleven-year-olds with licences,' laughed his mum.

As the O'Connells took off, two cars screeched onto the airfield. Evy's brother Jonathan was in the first. Two angry men, owed money by Jonathan, were in the second. Pleading to escape his creditors, Jonathan was allowed on board the balloon at the very last moment. The old team of Rick, Evy, Jonathan and Alex were heading back to Egypt and into more adventure!

This adventure was not long in coming! On their first visit to the ruined Temple of Hamunaptra, Jonathan fell through the floor, discovering a vault underneath. Amongst the rubble, Evy found an exquisite gold bracelet.

'It's the Manacle of Osiris,' explained Evy, excitedly. 'It's rumoured to have the power to move mountains, blot out the sun, set the seas aflame and resurrect the dead.'

'A Swiss army knife has nothing on this thing!' chuckled Rick.

Evy locked the magic bracelet in a box to take back to the British Museum. But, later that day, curiosity got the better of Alex. Left on his own, he took the Manacle out of the box and tried it on his wrist. FLASH! With a pulse of unearthly energy, the golden bracelet clamped itself round Alex's wrist! Then he experienced a vision of a stepped pyramid and being strapped down on a table.

Meanwhile, in another part of the gloomy temple, Colin Weasler arrived from London with The Book of the Dead under his arm. This Egyptian artefact with amazing powers had once brought Evy back to life. And Weasler had a similar plan.

'Time to rise and shine, my mummy friend,' he sniggered. 'I need you to settle a score for me!'

Chanting from the book in the burial chamber of Imhotep, Weasler succeeded in bringing the Mummy back to life. With scarab beetles pouring through his bandages, Imhotep reared up from his tomb and towered over the jealous assistant curator.

'I command you.' began Weasler.

'You command me?' roared Imhotep, sending the puny figure flying across the room in a burst of purple flame!

Snatching the Book of the Dead, Imhotep performed two further transformations. First, he assumed his human form. Then, with a horrible roar, he brought his skeleton guards back to life.

'The world condemned me to eternal suffering,' he told them. 'I only need the powers of the Manacle of Osiris to exact my revenge!'

Knowing that Evy had found the Manacle, Weasler led Imhotep straight to the family.

'Doesn't anybody ever stay dead around here? 'exclaimed Rick, suddenly finding himself confronted by his old enemy. Then Imhotep's skeleton soldiers attacked. The O'Connells would have lost the fight if it hadn't been for the timely arrival of Ardeth Bay, their old friend and leader of the forces against the Mummy.

'We've got to stop meeting like this!' quipped Rick, amidst the heat of battle.

Although the skeleton soldiers were defeated, Imhotep managed to kidnap Alex. Whirling like a mini tornado, the Mummy carried the boy and Weasler across the desert to the stepped Pyramid of Saqqara. Inside, Alex was strapped down onto a flat stone slab just as his vision had warned him!

'I'm preparing the boy for the separation ritual!' said Imhotep.

'Somehow, I don't like the sound of that!' gulped Alex.

Ardeth Bay knew the Mummy's plan. After Imhotep had removed the Manacle of Osiris, he would try to get hold of The Scrolls of Thebes.

'The Scrolls are an ancient instruction manual for the Manacle on Alex's wrist,' he explained.

'If Imhotep possesses both the Manacle and the Scrolls, the world will be forced to bow at the Mummy's feet!'

So the O'Connells followed in the Zephyr, desperate to save Alex and, with him, the world!

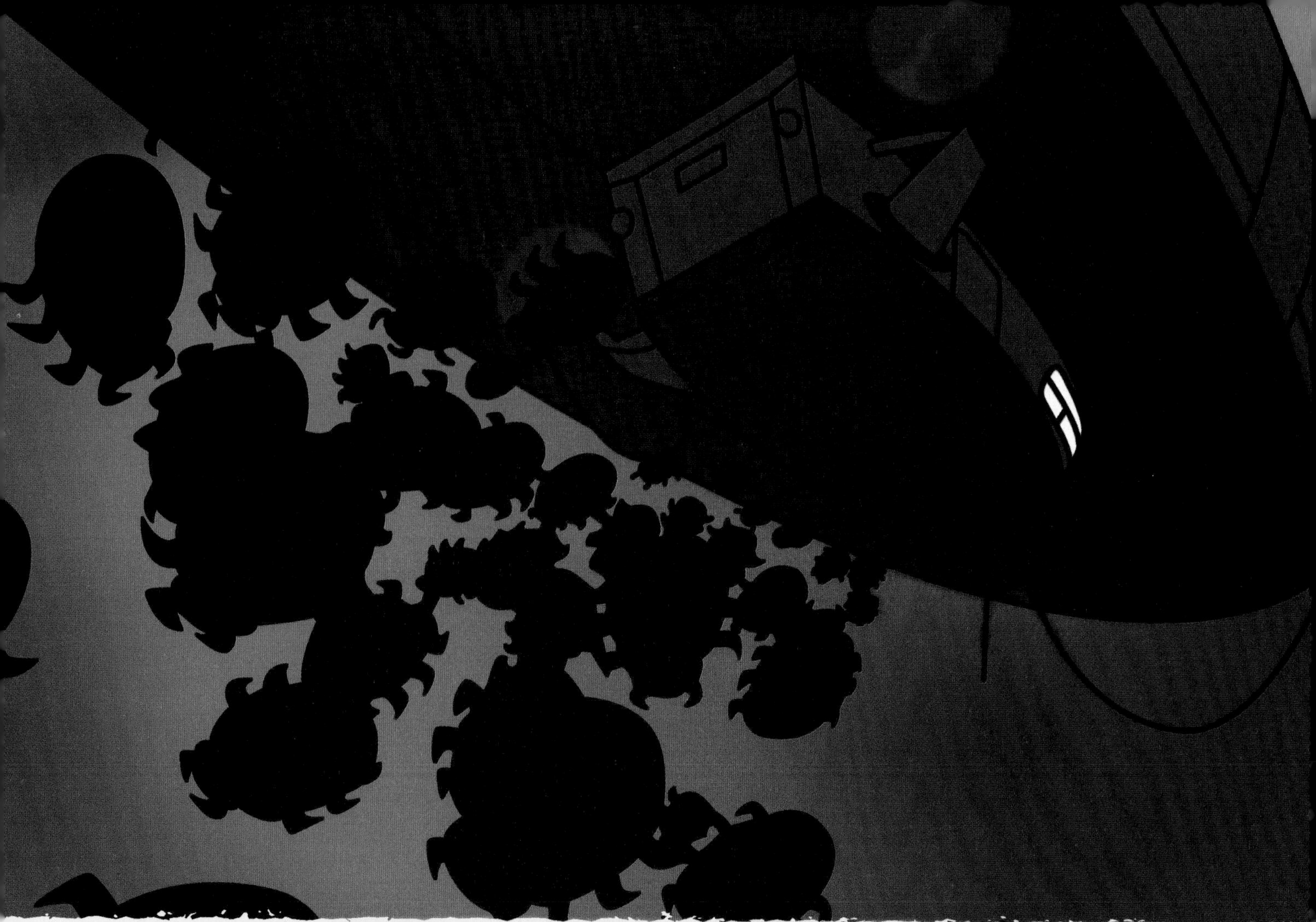

It proved a daunting task! Imhotep had all his powers back now and unleashed a scarab beetle at the approaching balloon. The beetle multiplied into a deadly black swarm that rapidly infested the cabin.

'They will devour everything in their path!' warned Ardeth Bay, flailing at the sea of insects with his sword.

The beetles threatened to bring the Zephyr down. So Rick expelled some with a cannister of gas and then plugged the hole they had made in the balloon skin with his bottom! Meanwhile, Evy used Jonathan as bait to lure the rest of the creatures over a trap door. Then she opened it and they tumbled from the balloon!

Barely under control, the Zephyr landed at the Pyramid of Saqqara. Hurrying inside, the O'Connells found Weasler searching a treasure-filled tomb for the Scrolls of Thebes.

'They've got to be here somewhere!' he cried, tossing the priceless relics aside like old jumble. Suddenly, he found himself confronted by Evy!

'Where is Alex?' she shouted, holding her ex-colleague over a deep shaft and fixing him with a furious mother's stare!

Weasler revealed that Alex was in the Grand Gallery with Imhotep.

'And the Scrolls?' demanded Ardeth Bay.

'They're not here, I swear!' screamed Weasler.

The family arrived at the Gallery in time to prevent the Mummy hurting Alex. But Imhotep was far from beaten.

'Arise my warriors!' he bellowed, as more skeleton soldiers burst up through the floor!

Another fight began. Again, the odds were so overwhelming that the forces of evil soon gained the upper hand. No sooner had the O'Connells defeated one skeleton soldier than two more took his place. Then, using his amazing supernatural strength, Imhotep picked up a huge stone statue and held it above his head, ready to crush everyone beneath him.

'Draw you last breath!' he chuckled.

Despite still being strapped to his slab, Alex came to the rescue. Waving his wrist, the Manacle of Osiris burst into life and sent waves of supernatural energy shooting in all directions. The skeleton soldiers disintegrated. The stone statue crumbed to dust above the Mummy's head, knocking him over. And Alex was freed from his bonds.

'Maybe this thing isn't so bad after all!' he chuckled.

It seemed the tide had turned. Grabbing The Book of the Dead, Evy began reciting some spells that would send the Mummy back to the Underworld. But she was stopped by Weasler before she could finish.

'Now Imhotep is caught somewhere between a mortal and undead!' she cried.

Worse was to follow. In the struggle with Weasler, The Book of the Dead fell over the edge of a cliff and was lost. Now the Mummy could never be banished again!

With a roar and a whirl of dust, Imhotep swept from the tomb. In the sudden silence, everyone realised what had happened and what the future held in store.

'I think Imhotep has decided to find the Scrolls of Thebes first,' said Evy.

'And then,' added Alex, grimly, 'he'll come back for the Manacle, won't he?'

SHADOWS IN THE TOMB

Deep underground, with only a flickering torch to light you, the only way to tell if someone's coming is from the shadows on the wall.
Are they friend or foe?

Practice your recognition skills by identifying these five silhouettes and writing the name of each person underneath.

Answers: 1.Alex 2.Rick 3.Ardeth Bay 4.Evy 5.Imhotep

JONATHON'S LITTLE

Jonathon Carnahan loves the riches of Antiquity. After all, he risked life and limb to snatch the huge diamond from the top of the Pyramid of Anubis!

Here are some more of Jonathan's special gems. Only this time they are sparkling snippets of information about Ancient Egypt. But be careful - only five of these items are true. The other three are totally false.

Can you spot the fakes?

1 There was a real man called Imhotep. He was extremely clever, excelling in poetry,philosophy and medicine. He was also a brilliant architect and was responsible for building the first stone pyramid, the Step Pyramid, about 2680 BC.

2 The Faraoe Islands in Scotland take their name from the Pharaohs. When the Romans invaded Egypt, they drove out the last of the Egyptian Kings who fled to these remote islands for safety.

3 Scarab beetles were revered by the Egyptians because they can both fly and burrow in the ground. So it was thought that they could move between this life and the afterlife.

GEMS

4 The meaning of Hieroglyphs, the system of Ancient Egyptian picture symbols, was not unravelled until 1799. Then, the Rosetta Stone was found. It contained parallel texts in Greek and Hieroglyph. So the Greek was used to 'translate' the pictures.

5 Egypt's largest pyramid, the Great Pyramid, is found at Giza. This ancient site beside the Nile gets its name from the first British explorer to visit there in 1746. When Sir Harvey Awadzi opened the tomb inside the Great Pyramid and saw the mummified body inside, he was heard to exclaim : 'Who's this geezer?'

6 Some scientists believe that the famous 'Curse Of Tutankhamen' may be based in fact. Many mummies, and the walls of their tombs, are a breeding ground for a deadly mould which, when inhaled, leads to organ failure and a painful death.

7 There really was a Book Of The Dead. It contained prayers to protect Ancient Egyptians in the afterlife and also passwords which they believed would speed them through the underworld.

8 Cleopatra invented the first type of scratch card. She was fond of burying some of her treasures in the sand and then getting servants to blow the sand away with giant feather fans. Mark Anthony enjoyed gambling on the outcome of this game.

Answers: The following items are false - numbers 2, 5 and 8

BEWARE THE UNDEAD!

Colour this picture of the O'Connells being attacked by one of Imhotep's mummified guards, using the inset picture to guide you.

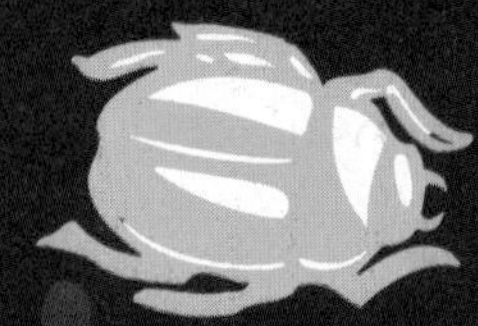

THE MUMMY™ THE ANIMATED SERIES

A CANDLE IN THE DARKNESS

In their base camp outside Alexandria, Alex was struggling with the Greek and Latin homework set by his mum. He complained bitterly about learning dead languages, but she turned a deaf ear to his protests.

"Knowledge is like a candle in the darkness," she explained, "lighting your way through life!" But, when Jonathan offered a trip into town on his motorbike, Alex jumped at the chance!

In the ancient city, the visitors found themselves outside a ruined library with a huge symbol of knowledge above the entrance.

"Never much cared for libraries," commented Jonathan. "All that "shhhushing", I suspect!" His words were drowned out by a sudden loud rumble that made everything shake.

"Earthquake!" yelled Alex.

Despite all the falling masonry, Alex and Jonathan escaped unharmed. Then the Manacle on his wrist gave Alex another vision. He saw a gold shield shimmering in the darkness. When the vision passed, he found that the earthquake had revealed a secret doorway into the ancient library. He persuaded Jonathan to go inside.

"What if the Scrolls of Thebes are in there?" cried Alex.

In the map room of the ruined building, Alex found a model of Ancient Alexandria. All the miniature buildings had special symbols written on them. So Alex made an accurate sketch of the model city, unaware they were being watched by Colin Weasler. And Weasler was now the servant of Imhotep!

The Mummy saw Alex and Jonathan trying to sneak out of the library.

"The Manacle!" he cried, catching sight of the thing he wanted most in the world on Alex's wrist. Dodging the exploding fireballs fired from Imhotep's fingertips, Alex and Jonathan managed to race outside. But Imhotep followed, bursting out through the ground with a terrifying roar.

Just a few feet away, Jonathan struggled to start his motorbike.

"Now would be a good time to go, Uncle Jonathan!" yelled Alex.

"Alex," retorted Jonathan, "you know I don't work well under pressure." Eventually, the old bike fired and they roared away. But the chase was on!

Using his incredible supernatural powers, Imhotep turned himself into a whirlwind that picked up everything in its path – including Weasler! With the Mummy's terrifying face at the centre of the whirlwind, Alex and Jonathan were pursued across the desert, just managing to stay ahead of their enemy.

"It's gaining on us! FASTER!" shouted Alex.

But the elderly motorbike was going at full throttle.

Then Jonathan spotted a river up ahead. He sped straight through it, spraying a huge sheet of water at the whirlwind. It broke up the vortex, dumping Weasler and Imhotep on the river bank.

"You did it! You saved us!" whooped Alex.

"You don't have to sound so amazed," replied Jonathan.

Back at base camp, Alex was told off for skipping his homework and Jonathan in trouble for leading the boy astray. But all this was quickly forgotten when Evy saw the sketch of the model.

"This building here, in the hills," she said. "It has the symbol of knowledge, just like on the Library. Could it be there's a second library...a secret annex?"

Maybe this was the hiding place of the Scrolls!

At first light next day, the Zephyr took off in search of the library annex. And it was not long before Alex's sharp eyes spotted what looked like the entrance in a canyon below. But their search did not go unnoticed. Standing on a nearby hilltop, Imhotep watched the O'Connells' every move – and his face broke into a cruel and evil smile!

The Zephyr landed in the canyon. Leaving Alex and Jonathan in the cabin, Evy and Rick went into the complex of caves. Then Alex spotted Weasler arriving with Imhotep. With Jonathan following, he ran inside to warn his parents.

Everyone met up in a dark chamber full of rolled up parchments.

"The Scrolls of Thebes!" demanded Imhotep.

"You didn't say 'pretty please'!" retorted Rick.

"We don't have to!" sneered Weasler.

The Mummy recited an ancient Egyptian spell and some terrifying, jackal-headed creatures appeared.

" Shadow Demons!" gasped Evy.

The Shadow Demons proved impossible to fight. When Rick threw a punch, his fist went through the creature's shadow body and hit the wall! Then Alex spotted that the demons were frightened of fire. So Rick used some flares he was carrying in a pouch round his waist to drive the monsters away.

The O'Connells hurried off in search of the Scrolls. They had not gone far when a trapdoor opened and Alex found himself hurtling down towards some razor-sharp spikes below. Rick dived after him and just managed to catch his son by using his bullwhip as a rope.

"Pretty exciting stuff for a library!" commented Alex, their feet safely on the ground again.

By now, Imhotep and his Shadow Demons had recovered. They followed Evy and Jonathan to the Fifth Dynasty room where the Scrolls might be hidden. When Rick and Alex joined them, the Mummy saw his prize within his grasp.

"The Scrolls and The Manacle," he growled. "How convenient!"

Imhotep and his creatures closed in. So Rick reached into his pouch for some more flares – but they had all gone!

The family was now in desperate trouble. But, suddenly, Alex's vision returned! He realised that the shield he had seen matched the shields around the wall of the room. Racing over to one of them, Alex used his limited knowledge of Greek to read an inscription. It told him to turn a wheel and pull a lever. Immediately, golden sunlight flooded the room. It flashed off the shields and dissolved the Shadow Demons away!

For the first time, Alex realised the value of ancient languages. But they were not out of danger yet – Imhotep and Weasler were still on the loose. As Evy searched frantically for the Scrolls, finding only a scrap of paper instead, the Mummy bore down on her like a deadly black crow.

This time, the Manacle came to the rescue. Radiating flashes of supernatural energy, it turned the scrolls and books on the library shelves into weapons. The scrolls flew down like birds and wrapped themselves round Imhotep so he could not see or move. And the books completely buried Weasler. Both their enemies were now defeated!

"The power of knowledge!" chuckled Rick.

Another earthquake started bringing the secret library crashing down. Fleeing outside, the family gathered round Evy to inspect paper she had found.

"It states that Alexander the Great himself checked out the Scrolls and never returned them," she murmured. "So we'll need to find Alexander's lost diaries. They could be almost anywhere. He travelled from Europe through China and into India."

"Guess this means I have a lot of studying to do," sighed Alex.

Meanwhile, trapped in the library ruins, Imhotep tore off the parchment binding him and glared furiously into the darkness.

"No one makes a fool out of Imhotep and lives!" he snarled.

IN AN EGYPTIAN BAZAAR

There are SIX SMALL DIFFERENCES between these two ancient market scenes. Can you spot them? (You'll need to look very carefully - some are not easy to find!)

Answers on page 50

THE POWER OF THE

How would you like to have Imotep's supernatural powers? Well, now you can!

Just solve these simple crossword-type clues and write your answers in the boxes opposite. You'll find that you make some AMAZING transformations!

MUMMY

Can you turn SAND into GOLD?

SAND

On the end of your wrist _ _ _ _
Plays music or a thin rubber circle _ _ _ _
No hair _ _ _ _
Very brave and fearless _ _ _ _

GOLD

Can you turn HEAT into COLD?

HEAT

Getting better, cured of an injury _ _ _ _
Place of fire inhabited by The Devil _ _ _ _
You do this with your hand - in the past! _ _ _ _
You do this with your hand - in the present! _ _ _ _

COLD

Can you turn ROCK into DUST?

ROCK

Another word for harbour or port _ _ _ _
Pack of card or floor of a ship _ _ _ _
You sit at one of these at school _ _ _ _
Just as it is getting dark _ _ _ _

DUST

Answers: 1.SAND HAND BAND BALD BOLD GOLD 2.ROCK DOCK DECK DESK DUSK DUST 3.HEAT HEAL HELL HELD HOLD COLD

ALEX'S PYRAMID

Like his mother Evy, Alex O'Connell loves all things Egyptian - especially solving the mysterious codes found in ancient tombs.

Here's an Egyptian-type coded puzzle that you can help Alex to solve.

First of all, complete the number pyramid. The number in each box is the sum of the two numbers underneath it - so add from the bottom upwards. When the pyramid is full, each number will have a matching letter. Use these to unlock the three coded messages.

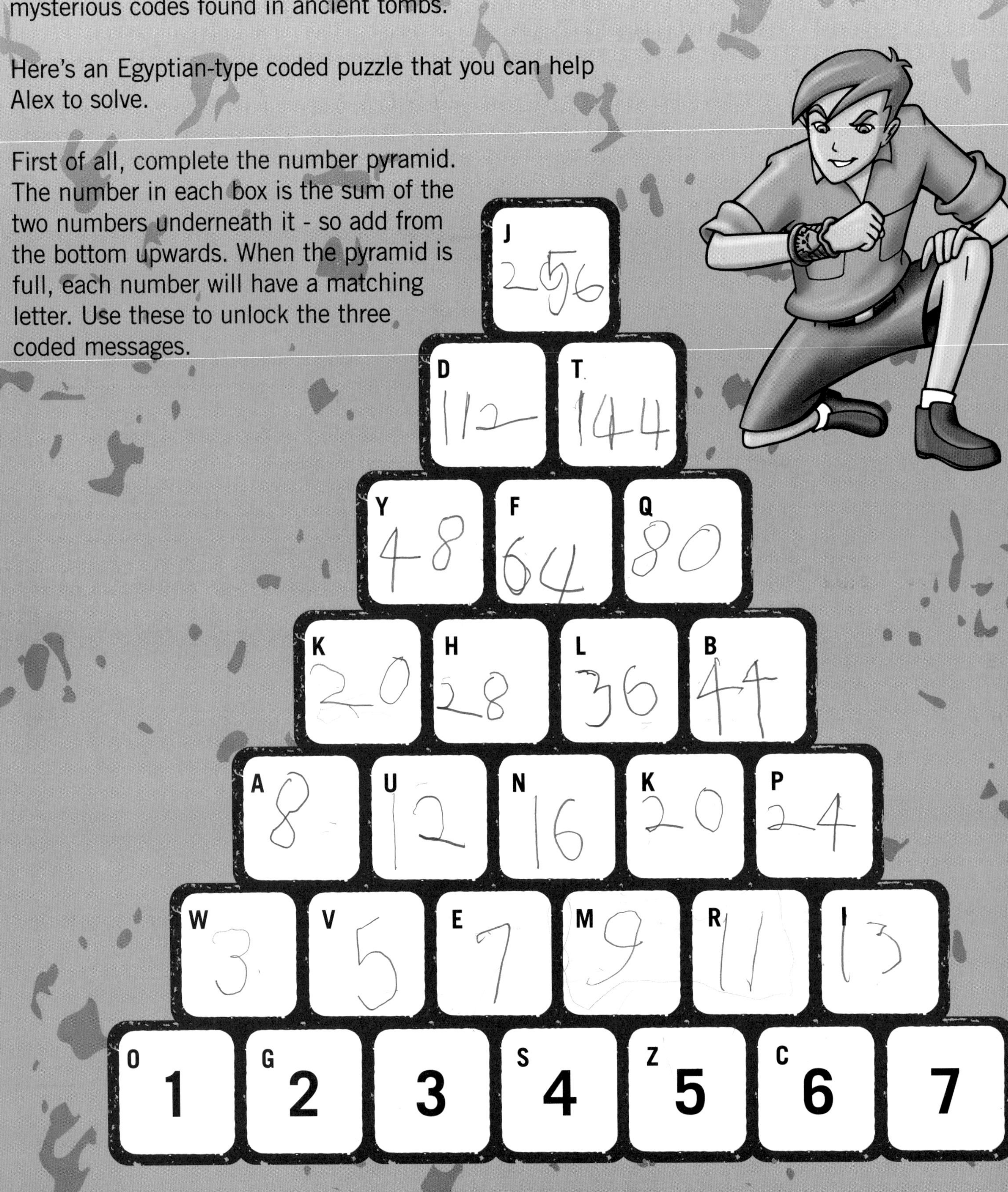

PUZZLE

Mum says:

Dad says:

112 1 16 144
3 13 144 28
9 1 11 7

9 7 4 4
8 16 48
8 11 9 44 8 16 112 4 !

Imhotep says:

13 4 28 8 36 36
11 7 144 12 11 16 !

Answers: 1.HAVE YOU DONE YOUR HOMEWORK?
2.DON'T MESS WITH ANY MORE ARMBANDS! 3.I SHALL RETURN!

ESCAPE FROM IMHOTEP

Many times you've seen the O'Connell family get away from The Mummy by the skin on their teeth. Now it is YOUR turn to know how it feels!

Only ONE PATH leads through this terror-filled tomb. Can you find it and escape the clutches of Imhotep?

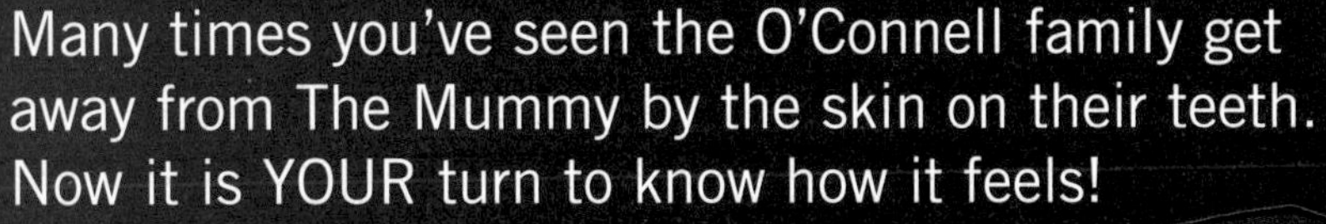

START HERE

Answers from page 43

AGAINST THE ELEMENTS

The O'Connell family were in India. They had found Alexander the Great's secret diary in an Indus temple. But the book was lost when Jonathan tried to steal a big green diamond from the forehead of a statue and the whole temple collapsed. Luckily, Alex had removed the relevant page first!

"I owe you one, mate!" whispered Jonathan.

Everyone gathered round as Evy translated the rescued sheet.

"The diary states," she said, excitedly, "that Alexander left the Scrolls of Thebes at the Palace of Merneptah in the ancient Egyptian city of Memphis for safekeeping."

That meant that the family had to travel back to Egypt - but the Zephyr was out of commission.

Rick and Evy went to find alternative means of transport, leaving Alex and Jonathan to look round an Indian bazaar. Suddenly a snake-charmer's cobra attacked Alex. He was saved by a mongoose who then leapt onto his shoulders and befriended him.

"I'm gonna call him Tut!" decided the boy. Alex was not allowed pets, so he kept Tut hidden in his bag. And Jonathan promised not to tell to return the favour he owed Alex.

To Jonathan's dismay, the transport turned out to be a team of elephants.

"You positive these things are safe?" he complained, struggling to climb into the saddle.

"Sure!" laughed Rick. "Just don't act like a peanut!"

The party set off for the long, slow walk from India to Egypt. Their departure was watched by Salah, an Indian spy employed by Colin Weasler.

Salah told Weasler and Imhotep that the search for the Scrolls had moved back to Egypt.

"Shouldn't we be going, master?" asked Weasler. "If the O'Connells get to the palace first..."

"Their progress will be slowed!" growled the Mummy. Imhotep opened a chest to reveal a gold staff covered in jewels.

"The Staff of Set!" gasped Weasler. "With it, you'll be able to control the elemental forces of nature!"

By now, the family had reached the River Nile. They were making their way downstream on an old wooden barge. Tut's presence kept making Rick sneeze, but Alex continued to keep him a secret. And it seemed that the river trip would prove uneventful until Imhotep unleashed the awesome powers of his ancient staff.

Set was the Egyptian god of chaos. Whoever owned his staff could control the four basic elements of earth, wind, fire and water. Imhotep chose water, causing a huge Water Dragon with his own terrifying face to rear up behind the O'Connell's boat.

"Dive!" yelled Rick.

Everyone flung themselves into the river as the water-creature crashed down on them.

There was no escape from the creature. As they struggled back onto their half-sunk barge, the Dragon turned into a waterspout that lifted Rick into the air. As he splashed down into the river, the beast transformed again into a violent whirlpool that sucked Rick under. When his waving hand disappeared for the last time, Evy and the others thought he was lost!

Help arrived at the very last minute in the form of Ardeth Bay. The brave and clever Med-Jai warrior fired an arrow at the barge. Then, with a rope tied to the arrow, he used his horse to pull the boat along. Alex managed to steer it close to the whirlpool so that Rick could be rescued.

"I need a desk job," spluttered Rick, scrambling back on board.

Leaving the Nile behind, the O'Connells and Ardeth Bay travelled overland to the Palace of Merneptah in Memphis. Using dynamite to blast a way to the entrance, they were about to go in search of the Scrolls when another sneezing fit led to the discovery of Tut.

"I can explain..." began Alex.

"We'll talk about this later!" snapped Rick.

Imhotep stood watching as Rick and Ardeth Bay prised open the Palace door. Then, with his Staff of Set, he brought the gigantic stone statues guarding the entrance to life.

"Stone Mummies!" gasped Evy. "The Earth elementals!"

The O'Connells were helpless against these enormous creatures. As they were flung around like rag dolls, Imhotep told Weasler to bring Alex inside.

"We will separate him from the Manacle of Osiris!" he growled.

Leaving Ardeth Bay and Jonathan to battle with the Stone Mummies, Alex and Evy rushed into the Palace to rescue their son. The Mummy's response was to unleash the third awesome power on his enemies.

"Great Staff," he chanted in Ancient Egyptian, "I summon a Wind Demon!"

Like the Water Dragon before it, the Wind Demon bore the same ugly, snarling face of the Mummy. Swirling through the stone corridors of the Palace, it sucked Rick and Evy right off their feet. As they disappeared into the cyclone, Alex realised he had to act. So, pushing backwards, he managed to knock Weasler out and get free.

Using two belts strapped together, Alex reached out to his parents and gave them something to grab hold of. But he did not have the strength to pull them clear of the raging whirlwind. Then the bracelet on Alex's wrist flashed into life. It created a powerful vacuum that sucked the Wind Demon away, leaving his mum and dad safe.

"Sometimes, you gotta love that Manacle!" chuckled Rick.

Outside, Jonathan and Ardeth Bay succeeded in destroying the Stone Mummies with the rest of Rick's dynamite. So, with three of his elemental forces now overcome, Imhotep turned to the fourth – the element of Fire.

"Soon the fate of the world will be sealed!" he roared, drumming the Staff of Set on the ground and producing two Fire Hounds. These giant dogs, like enormous wolves, were made entirely of flames!

The fiery creatures chased Rick and Evy from pillar to post. Rick kept one at bay by jamming a vase over its head. And Evy choked the other by giving it a stone ball to fetch. But it was obvious they could not escape for ever.

"Need a little help here, buddy!" Alex said to Tut.

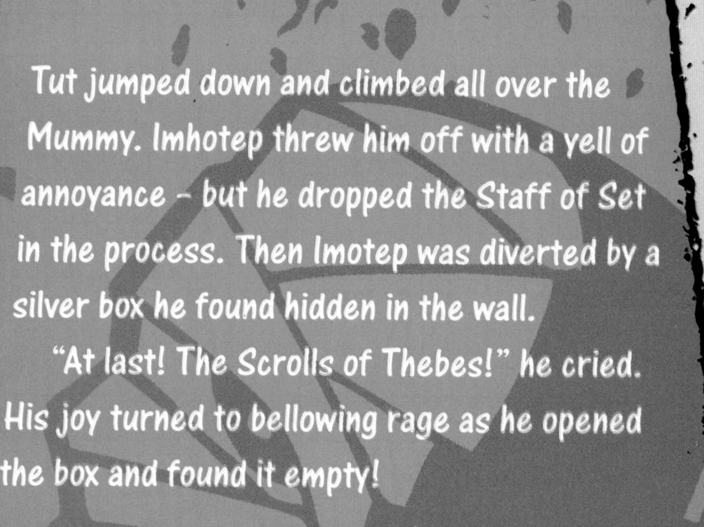

Tut jumped down and climbed all over the Mummy. Imhotep threw him off with a yell of annoyance – but he dropped the Staff of Set in the process. Then Imotep was diverted by a silver box he found hidden in the wall.

"At last! The Scrolls of Thebes!" he cried. His joy turned to bellowing rage as he opened the box and found it empty!

Now Alex had what he needed to defeat the Mummy. Brandishing the Staff and chanting some Ancient Egyptian he had remembered from his studies, he ordered to Fire Hounds to attach Imhotep instead.

"Next time, you will not be so lucky!" he snarled, turning into sand and seeping away under the wall. Alex finished the job by smashing the Staff of Set, causing the Hounds to disappear in two puffs of smoke!

At last, the danger was over – but Jonathan still found something to complain about.

"No scrolls?" he exclaimed, looking into the empty box. "You mean I was almost drowned, trampled and barbecued…and the Scrolls aren't even here?"

"Where to now?" asked Rick.

"We follow Alexander's path : Greece…Armenia…Asia Minor. Wherever we have to go to find the next clue."

Suddenly, Tut appeared on Rick's shoulder, reminding everyone that his future was still undecided.

"How about it, dad?" asked Alex, hopefully. "Can I keep him?"

"I think he's earned his keep," replied Rick with a smile. "Good friends are hard to find!"

"What about your sneezing fits?" murmured Evy.

"If I can get used to Jonathan," chuckled Rick, "I can get used to anything!"